CHAPTER
1

"**N**o problem, Mom, no problem."

"Oliver, I'm not sure you've understood me. It *will* be a problem unless we get this straight."

Oliver knew his mother meant business. He looked as serious as he knew how. "I do understand, Mom. You're saying only one customer at a time."

"One, count 'em, *one* at a time. No exceptions. We've had a garage full of gerbils, guinea pigs, tropical fish, rabbits, and even an ape—"

"It was a rhesus monkey, Mom."

"Whatever. Whatever it was, it was too much. It was too much for me and too much for poor Pom-pom."

Pom-pom was the reason Oliver started the pet-sitting business in the first place.

Oliver had begged his mother for a dog of his own, a dog he could pet and feed and take on long walks through the woods. And what did they get instead? A frisky little Shih Tzu that slept on a silk pillow on Mrs. Moffitt's bed.

Pom-pom had pink ribbons tied in his mop of hair. He was even fed grapes from the table. One at a time—and peeled!

Pom-pom was hardly Oliver's idea of a dog, but Mrs. Moffitt really loved him, so Oliver guessed the mop-dog probably wasn't so bad.

"Okay, Mom, I promise. This summer there'll be only one customer at a time."

"Well, that's a relief." Mrs. Moffitt paused. "I know you're good at your business—I'll bet you're the best pet-sitter in town. It's just that sometimes . . . well, sometimes you get a little carried away."

"Not this summer, Mom. This summer I'm strictly One-at-a-Time Oliver."

"Good." Mrs. Moffitt kissed One-at-a-Time Oliver on his forehead. "Supper will be ready in half an hour."

Oliver lay on his bed thinking about the summer. "Looks like it's gonna be a rough one. School's been out for a week, I'm flat broke, I don't have even one customer lined up and the phone hasn't rung for ages."

The phone rang.

Oliver bounced across the bed and picked it up in such a hurry that he grabbed the wrong end of the receiver.

"Hello," he said into the earpiece. "Oliver's Pet-Care Service. I'm good with dogs and good with cats. I'll even baby-sit your rats. May I help you?"

From the part of the receiver by his mouth, he heard, "Oliver, is that you? Why do you sound so far away?"

Oliver felt himself blushing. "Hold on a minute," he shouted into the wrong end of the phone. He turned the receiver right side up and said, "Sorry about that, Sam."

Samantha Lawrence was Oliver's next-door neighbor and best friend. She was also the best athlete in their class and the fastest runner in the school. "What's up?" Sam said.

"Well, Mom just read me the riot act about my business. I'm only allowed to take on one customer at a time. To tell you the truth, at this point I'd be grateful for just one customer. Oliver's Pet-Care Service is temporarily bankrupt."

"Have you tried advertising?"

"Sure have. Josh cranked out a whole new batch of handbills on his computer, and we passed them out at school the week before vacation. But I didn't get a single phone call."

Josh Burns was another one of Oliver's friends. He was also the smartest kid in the class and a whiz with computers.

Sam thought a minute. "Maybe you should try a different kind of advertising."

"What do you mean, Sam?"

"Maybe you should put an ad in the paper."

"We tried that, and—"

"No, not the school paper. A grown-up paper. How about the *Chronicle*?"

"Hey! That's a great . . . no, it wouldn't work."

"Why not?"

9

" 'Cause ads cost money, and money is something I don't have."

Sam laughed. "Well, as you always say, 'No problem.' "

Oliver scratched his head. "Why is it no problem?"

"Because I'll lend you the money. I have some birthday money my grandma sent me. You can pay me back as soon as you get your first customer."

"Thanks, Sam. You're a pal."

The next morning, as soon as the breakfast dishes were dried and put away, Oliver grabbed his bike and raced over to Sam's house.

Sam was doing sit-ups on the porch. When she saw Oliver, she leaped over the porch rail and hopped lightly onto her bike. Together, she and Oliver rode to Josh's house.

Mrs. Burns opened the door. "Hello, Oliver. Hello, Samantha. How are you this morning?"

Oliver answered. "Fine, Mrs. Burns. Is Josh home?"

"He and Matthew are upstairs." Mrs. Burns looked puzzled. "They said something about karate and computers."

Oliver grinned. "I'll bet Matthew is taking computer lessons now." Matthew Farley's parents were always sending him off for lessons to "improve himself." He had taken trumpet lessons, chess lessons, tennis lessons, and karate lessons.

Josh and Matthew were huddled around the monitor when Sam and Oliver walked in. On

the screen, two stick figures stood facing each other. Josh typed something on the keyboard and pressed the "Return" key. One of the stick figures reached up with his stick arm and suddenly flattened the other stick figure. The computer went *Boiiing!*

"Got him!" Matthew shouted.

"Got who?" Sam asked.

The boys looked up from the screen. "Hi, Sam. Hi, Oliver," Josh answered. "We're just working out some karate moves for Matthew for the fair. I'm his consultant."

"What fair?" asked Oliver.

"The county fair," Matthew answered. "It's coming up pretty soon, and my karate team is putting on an exhibition. Josh and I are planning out my strategy on the computer. Do you want to help?"

"Well," said Sam, "we were about to ask *you* for help."

"Sure, what's the problem?" Josh asked.

"The problem is that Oliver's broke. He needs customers, and the handbills you guys passed out aren't bringing in any business."

"One customer," Oliver added quickly. "I'm allowed only one customer at a time."

"You're not going to get much money from one customer," said Matthew.

Josh pressed a key on the computer and several more stick figures appeared on the screen. He pressed another key. Suddenly, one of the figures started kicking and punching. It kicked and punched the others until it was the only figure left standing. The computer went *Boing!*

Boiiing! Boiiing! BOIIIING! Josh jumped up and down in his chair. "That's it, Matthew! That's how you're going to do it!"

Matthew studied the screen. "Do you really think so, Josh?"

Sam gave a polite cough. "Hey, guys. That's all very interesting, but it doesn't help Oliver with his problem, which is what we came here to talk about in the first place. Remember?"

"Oh, yeah," said Josh. "Sorry, Oliver. You said you needed a customer?"

"Yeah. But I can have only one, so I guess it should be a big one. Got any ideas?"

Josh and Matthew shook their heads.

"I think Oliver should put an ad in the *Chronicle*," Sam suggested. "There must be some rich pet owners who read the *Chronicle*," Matthew said.

Josh agreed. "Good idea. Let's write the ad now." He cleared the karate figures from the screen, slipped in a new disk, and together, the four friends wrote the ad:

CATS! RATS! BATS!
GIVE YOUR PET A SUMMER VACATION AT
OLIVER'S PET-CARE SERVICE.
NO PET TOO BIG OR TOO SMALL.
CALL 555-8085 TODAY!

Then they delivered the ad to the *Chronicle* office, paid for it, and set off on their bikes for the Quick Shoppe.

Kim Williams, Jennifer Hayes, and Kim's

brother, Parnell, were already at the Quick Shoppe, sitting in a big, round booth. They were drinking sodas, eating ice cream, and talking about the fair. As Oliver, Josh, Matthew, and Sam squeezed in, Parnell was explaining his entry in the Most Unusual Pet Contest. "You see," he said, "a boa constrictor is an unusual pet, but I was afraid it might not be unusual enough. Suppose somebody else enters a pet ostrich or a polar bear? So I decided to train Squeeze Me to do tricks. That way, he'll not only *be* unusual, but he'll *act* unusual too."

Jennifer shuddered. "I think having a snake for a pet is perfectly revolting. It gives me the creeps." Jennifer and Parnell's sister, Kim, were best friends. Whenever Jennifer went to the Williams' house, she stayed far away from Parnell's room, where Squeeze Me lived in a cage. "And besides, Parnell, a snake can't do tricks."

"Oh, yes, he can. I made an obstacle course and—"

"Come on, Parnell. An obstacle course? Out of what?"

"Paper-towel tubes and milk cartons and a shoe box with holes cut in the ends. I'm teaching Squeeze Me to run—uh, slither the course when I put him in the starting gate."

The whole gang looked doubtful until Kim added, "He *is* training Squeeze Me. I've watched."

"What are *you* doing for the fair, Kim?" Josh asked.

Kim put her arm around Jennifer. "We're entering the Big Bake-off. I'm baking something traditional—"

14

"Not me," interrupted Jennifer. "I'm baking something totally new. It's my own creation." She looked around the group. "If everybody promises not to tell, I'll let you in on what it is."

Everybody promised.

"It's a Purple Worms pie!"

"Oh, yuck!" said Matthew, looking as if he were about to be sick. "What are you going to do—get worms and dye them purple?"

"Don't be an idiot, Matthew! It's named the Purple Worms pie after my favorite rock group, the Purple Worms. It doesn't have real worms in it. I wouldn't touch a real worm any more than I'd touch Parnell's snake."

Jennifer loved the color purple. She dressed in purple, she dreamed in purple, and her cat, Princess Fluffy, always wore a purple ribbon.

"What is in it?" asked Sam.

"That's a secret. You'll see when it gets first prize at the fair. What about you, Sam? What are you doing?"

Sam looked thoughtful. "I don't know. I don't have an unusual pet, and I can't bake." She paused, then continued. "But when I heard Parnell talking about that obstacle course, it gave me an idea. Are there any obstacle courses or races for people?"

"There's a three-legged race," Parnell replied.

"Hmmm. A three-legged race." Sam thought for a minute. Then she snapped her fingers. "Yes, I am going to do something for the fair. I'm going to enter the three-legged race. And," she added mysteriously, "I know just who I'll get for a partner."

Oliver slurped the last of his ice-cream soda. Listening to all his friends plan for the fair made him want to enter a contest, too, but he couldn't think of anything to enter. Not one thing. "Guess I'd better go home and walk Pompom," he said. "Mom gets mad if I forget him."

Josh patted Oliver on the back. "You'll think of something to do for the fair, Oliver. There's still plenty of time."

The whole gang followed Oliver out of the Quick Shoppe. He was already feeling bad, but he was about to feel even worse.

Standing right outside the Quick Shoppe was his number-one enemy, Rusty Jackson, with his sidekicks, Jay Goodman and Paul Patterson. Rusty was holding a large slice of watermelon. Jay and Paul were each holding empty tin cans. Rusty took a big bite from the watermelon and spit the seeds at the tin cans. Some of the seeds landed on Jay's arm, some on Paul's hand, but most landed on the ground.

"Hey, Moffitt," Rusty yelled with his mouth full of watermelon. "Wanna enter the Great Watermelon Seed-Spitting Contest?" He blew a seed in Oliver's direction. It landed right on Oliver's shoe. Rusty laughed. "Oh, a thousand pardons, Moffitt. I didn't think it would go that far."

Oliver wiped off the seed with his other shoe. "I'll bet you didn't, Rusty," he muttered.

"So, Moffitt, what contest are you entering at the fair? You won't have a chance against me in the seed-spitting contest. But you could always

enter your doggy. It would be a sure win if there's a contest for the nerdiest pet in town!'' Rusty and his sidekicks bellowed with laughter.

"You can laugh all you want now, Rusty. But the last laugh will be mine!"

"I'm shaking, Moffitt. I'm really shaking," Rusty said with a snicker.

Oliver turned and walked toward home. "I'd better think of something quick," he said to himself. "I've got to do something. But what?"

CHAPTER 2

Oliver didn't sleep well that night. He kept waking up with clenched fists and muttering, "I should have said ..." But before he could say what he should have said, he fell back into a fitful sleep.

When the phone beside his bed rang at 6:30 the next morning, he pulled the pillow over his head. But the phone kept ringing until Oliver reached out from under his pillow and picked up the receiver. " 'Lo," he mumbled in a sleepy voice.

"Are you the fella that put an ad in the paper about takin' care of animals?"

"What?"

"Are you the fella ..."

Suddenly Oliver was wide awake. "Yes! Yes, an ad about animals! Yes, that's me, Oliver's Pet-Care Service. I'm good with dogs and good with cats. I'll even baby-sit your rats. May I help you?"

"If you can come to the Morley farm on the Barton road in half an hour, maybe you can help me. And maybe I can help you."

"Yes, sir. Half an hour. The Barton farm on the Morley road. I'll be there."

"No, you won't."

"I—I won't?"

"Nope."

"Er . . . why won't I?"

"Because there's no such farm as the Barton farm and there's no such road as the Morley road. I *said*, 'Come to the Morley farm on the Barton road.' It's just past the fairgrounds." The voice chuckled. "You got the half-hour part right, so you can't be entirely asleep."

Oliver threw on his clothes and dashed down the stairs and out the back door. He leaped onto his bike and started pedaling as fast as he could.

To get to the Morley farm on the Barton road, which he now had straight, Oliver had to pass two places.

The first was Rusty's house. Oliver was grateful that the pest would be sound asleep this early in the morning, but he coasted silently by, just to make sure.

The second place was the fairgrounds. As Oliver biked toward the grounds, he saw workmen getting ready to give the red stables a new coat of paint. When he passed the entrance, he noticed a freshly painted sign. He slowed down and read:

**COME TO
THE COUNTY FAIR!
CONTESTS AND PRIZES
GALORE!
THRILLING ENTERTAINMENT
AND CAVALCADES!
FUN FOR ALL AGES!**

Pedaling on toward the Morley farm, Oliver wished and wondered. He wished he had a contest to enter, and he wondered what a cavalcade was.

Half a mile down the Barton road, Oliver came to a mailbox with W AND P MORLEY printed in black letters on its side. He turned up the dusty lane beside the mailbox and pedaled until he reached an old farmhouse and, across the land from it, a big red barn.

Both the house and the barn looked tidy but in need of paint, and the green tractor in the barnyard seemed to be almost an antique. Oliver leaned his bike against the white picket fence (which, he thought, also hadn't seen new paint for some time) in front of the house and started up the path toward the front door. He hadn't taken two steps, when a voice from the barn called, "Where you goin'?"

Oliver turned and saw a man in overalls standing beside the tractor. He had a wrench in one hand and a hammer in the other. "I—I'm going to see about a job," he answered.

"Would this job be takin' care of animals by any chance?"

"Yes, sir, it would."

"Well, do you think we keep our animals in the house?"

Oliver paused for a moment, scratched his head, then answered, "I guess that depends on what kind of animals you had in mind."

The farmer let out a big, hearty laugh which started in his belly and worked upward. When his laugh slowed down enough for him to talk, he said, "I guess you'll do." Dropping his wrench and hammer beside the tractor, he motioned for Oliver to follow him. "Now, come on over to this here barn," he called out behind him, "and meet the animals I did have in mind."

On the way into the barn the man introduced himself as Wendell Morley and explained that he and his wife, Priscilla, were about to leave on a trip to meet their newborn granddaughter. "I had a fella who was gonna look after my animals, but he up and got 'pendicitis. Until I saw your ad in the paper, I thought we wouldn't be able to go. Follow me. I'll show you around."

Mr. Morley pushed open the door to the barn. When Oliver stepped inside, he almost passed out!

The barn was filled with calves and cows, but it wasn't the sight of them that made Oliver's knees go weak. It was their smell!

"Somethin' the matter?"

"Uh—dno," said Oliver, breathing through his mouth.

Mr. Morley smiled. "Oh," he said, "I thought it might be the barn smell. It gets to a lot of people the first time they smell it. And sometimes, the second time too. But after a while you get used to it. Then it starts to smell sweet and natural to you, and you kinda miss it when you're not in the barn."

Oliver found it hard to imagine such a time, but he kept breathing through his mouth until he felt better.

Mr. Morley was already explaining what he'd have to do. "You needn't worry about the heifers 'cause tomorrow I'm turnin' them out to pasture. Understand?"

"Uh, dnod exagtly. Whad's a heifer?"

"Do you have a cold?"

"Dno, sir."

"Hay fever?"

"Dno, sir."

"Allergic to cows?"

"I don'd tink so."

"Then why in thunder are you talkin' like you've got a bee up your nose?"

Oliver realized that he was still breathing through his mouth. He inhaled one small breath through his nose, found that he could just stand the smell without passing out, and started to breathe normally. "Sorry, Mr. Morley. I'm all right now."

"Yes. Good. Well, heifers. Heifers are the big ones. We don't call 'em cows until after they've had a calf. But when they're too big to be calves themselves, that's when they become heifers. Got that?"

"Got it."

"Well, like I was sayin', the heifers will be on their own startin' tomorrow. But the calves still need lookin' after. That means comin' twice a day, once in the morning and once in the evening, and feedin' 'em, cleanin' 'em, and beddin' 'em down. Now, is that somethin' you can do?"

Oliver snapped to attention. "Yes, sir. As my ad says, No Pet—uh, Animal—Too Big or Too Small for Oliver's Pet-Care Service."

"Now you're talkin', son. Come around this evening, and I'll show you how to do chores."

"I'll be here."

While Mr. Morley was teaching Oliver the difference between cows, calves, and heifers, Sam was training for the three-legged race with five-year-old Andrew Finch. Mrs. Finch had asked Sam to baby-sit for Andrew three afternoons a week during the summer. Sometimes Sam thought Andrew was a nuisance. But that changed when she got the idea of entering the three-legged race with him.

Sam tied her leg to Andrew's with a strip of old sheet. "Okay, Andrew," she said. "Let's go!"

24

Sam took off. Andrew didn't. He fell flat on his face, pulling Sam down to the ground beside him. Andrew pouted and stamped his free foot. "I don't wanna race. I want my mommy."

Sam helped Andrew to his feet and brushed the dirt off his hands. "C'mon, Andrew. Remember the jelly beans I promised you?" Sam asked.

"Jelly beans! Hooray!" yelled Andrew.

"Okay. You can have a few jelly beans now. But then we have to practice. You want to enter the contest at the fair, don't you, Andrew?" asked Sam.

Andrew nodded and tossed the jelly beans quickly into his mouth.

Sam tied the strip of sheet around their legs with a double knot. "Now Andrew, when I say 'three,' you run. Okay?"

"Okay," said Andrew.

Sam held Andrew's hand tightly. "Ready? One. Two. Three. Go!"

Again Sam took off, but Andrew didn't. Sam and Andrew landed in a heap on the ground.

Andrew began to wail like a wolf howling at the moon.

Sam clasped one hand over his mouth, and, with the other, reached into her pocket. She pulled out another handful of jelly beans. "Here, Andrew. Please stop crying." Andrew stuck all the jelly beans into his mouth and smiled a big, juicy smile.

"This is all I can take for today," Sam thought as she untied the sheet. "I'm stuck with Andrew

for the summer—and for the three-legged race. I really want to win, but I don't stand a chance with Andrew as my partner. He's too short and too slow." She stood up and took Andrew's hand. "How can I make you taller and faster in time for the county fair?"

Andrew grinned. "More jelly beans?"

Sam sighed and shook her head.

That evening, as Oliver was leaving the house, his mother stopped him at the back door. "I noticed you were up early this morning," Mrs. Moffitt said to him.

Oliver smiled. "Yes, Mom, I finally got a job."

"Good. But I hope you remember," she said, "one customer at a time."

"I know, Mom," Oliver answered quickly. "But right now I've gotta go. If I don't learn the ropes real soon, I'll miss out on my only customer."

When he reached the farm, Oliver headed straight into the barn. He sniffed cautiously and was relieved to find he didn't feel like passing out. Maybe Mr. Morley was right.

"Mr. Morley!" Oliver called. "Are you in here?"

A heifer turned her big black-and-white face toward Oliver. At the same time, Oliver heard, "He's over here." Oliver laughed. "You know, cow," he said, "you sound a lot like a certain farmer I know."

From behind the heifer, Oliver heard Mr. Morley's belly laugh. When it settled down, the farmer's head popped up from over the animal's back. "Didn't fool ya, eh? Well, come on over to the calves, and I'll show you what needs doin'."

Mr. Morley led Oliver over to the calves. "Here they are. All thirteen of 'em. Aren't they beauties?"

"Thirteen?" repeated Oliver. "Did you say thirteen, Mr. Morley?"

"Yep, that's what I said."

"Uh-oh," Oliver thought, remembering the conversation with his mother. "First I have no customers, and now I have thirteen! What will Mom say when I tell her about this? Wait a minute . . . Mr. Morley is my customer, not the calves. He is just one customer, after all. And as long as I'm not bringing his thirteen calves home, Mom shouldn't mind at all! She'll probably be proud of me for taking on such a tough assignment. Right? Right. No problem."

All the while Oliver was talking to himself, Mr. Morley was talking to the calves. "They all know me," he said. "And they'll know you, too, after you've taken care of 'em for a few days. Follow me. I'll show you what to do."

Mr. Morley showed Oliver how to pull the strings off a bale of hay and how to feed slices of the bale to the calves. He showed him how to give a dishful of grain to each calf. "This is special grain for the little ones. It's called calf starter, and you get it out of that bag over there."

Next he showed Oliver where the bag of powdered milk was kept and how to mix a big

scoop of it with warm water in a pail. He showed him how to feed it to the calves.

The last calf, Number 13, was still too young to drink from the regular pail, so Mr. Morley poured the white liquid into a special pail with a nipple near the bottom. "This is a nipple pail, and this little lady will be drinking from it for the rest of the week." After much mooing and some grabs at the air, Number 13 latched onto the nipple and began sucking for all she was worth.

After the feeding Mr. Morley showed Oliver how to hoe off the manure into the gutter behind the calves. "Got to keep you little ladies neat and tidy," he said to the thirteen calves.

When the stalls were all cleaned, Mr. Morley spread a thick layer of fresh sawdust under each calf. "Gives 'em a nice clean bed to lie on," he said. When he was finished, Mr. Morley turned to Oliver. "Got all that, son?"

"I think so. Hay, calf starter, powdered milk—"

"Don't forget the special pail for Number Thirteen."

"Right. Then hoeing and sawdusting, and that's all there is to it."

"That's it. Think you can do it?"

"Yes, sir, I do. When do I start?"

"Tomorrow morning."

"Tomorr—tomorrow morning?"

"Bright and early. Any questions?"

Suddenly Oliver felt nervous. He'd expected a longer apprenticeship than one day. He thought furiously for questions. Then he realized he had two big ones. "Uh, yes, sir. First, how long will you be gone?"

Mr. Morley sighed. "Two weeks. It's been a long time since we got away from the place for even a night. I'm sure lookin' forward to goin', but I have to admit, I hate to miss the fair."

"You mean the county fair?"

"Sure do. I was lookin' forward to showin' my calves in the cavalcade."

"What is a cavalcade?"

"It's the parade of animals around the ring so the judges can pick the winners. They give out prizes for the best animals. I sure hate to miss it because I've got some mighty nice calves, especially that Number Thirteen. She's young and small, but she's a pretty little Holstein—"

"A pretty little Holstein?"

Mr. Morley laughed. "You don't know a Holstein from a Jersey, do you, son?"

Oliver felt his cheeks getting red from embarrassment. "I don't think so, Mr. Morley."

"Well, no reason you should. See how my herd is all black and white?" The farmer swept his hand through the air. "Well, they're Holsteins. If they were all light brown, they'd be Jerseys."

"Are Holsteins better than Jerseys?"

Again Mr. Morley laughed his deep belly laugh. "All depends on what you like. Me, I've always liked Holsteins. And that Number Thirteen ..." He clicked his tongue. "I had big hopes for her at the fair. If she won a ribbon, it'd be mighty good for the farm."

"Why is that?"

"The value of the animal is raised if it wins a prize at the fair. And we could sure do with a little prize-winnin' around here." Mr. Morley shook his head. "Kind of rough time for farming right now. Any other questions?"

"Well, we haven't talked about pay."

"Yep, that's true." Mr. Morley absent-mindedly rubbed the head of the heifer he was standing next to. "Well," he said, "Mrs. Morley and I were talkin' it over at dinnertime, and we decided the only fair thing was to pay you full wages, just as if you were bigger."

Full wages! Oliver nearly jumped for joy. His money problems were over! But then something in the farmer's expression brought him back down to earth. He remembered the lack of paint on the house and barn, and he thought of the ancient-looking tractor. His heart, which had been as light as a balloon, now felt a little heavy.

"Umm . . . I, uh, wonder . . ."

"What's on your mind, son? Spit it out."

Oliver had trouble getting the words out of his mouth. "Well, maybe I don't need full wages. I'm not full-size, and I'm just learning about taking care of calves."

Mr. Morley continued stroking the cow. "That's real good of you to offer, son. I have to admit, things have been tough around here for the last few years. And I was kinda hopin' to get a ribbon at the fair—that woulda helped. But Mrs. Morley said it, and I agree—if you hire somebody to do a full-size job, you gotta

pay full-size wages. And that's just what I in-
tend to do."

The two of them solemnly shook hands and
walked out of the barn, side by side.

CHAPTER
3

The next morning Oliver was up before the sun rose over the horizon. As he biked toward the farm, he noticed how peaceful and still the world was at that hour. "I ought to get up early more often," he thought. Then he remembered that he *would* be getting up early more often—every day for the next two weeks, in fact.

All was quiet as he glided past Rusty's, but at the fairgrounds, workers were busy. With paintbrushes and brooms they were preparing the place for the county fair. Oliver wished he could enter a contest, but again, he couldn't think of what to enter. Besides, he was going to be pretty tied up with thirteen calves to look after.

When Oliver reached the farm, there was a note waiting for him on the barn door. It read:

Dear Oliver,

It is 6:00 A.M. and we're just about ready to hit the road. Good luck with the calves. I know you'll do a good job because you're a nice young man. Remember: Hay, calf starter, powdered milk, hoe, sawdust—and don't forget the nipple pail.

Well, got to go now.
Good luck!

Wendell Morley

Oliver smiled to himself as he pushed open the barn door. Along with the smell, he was greeted by a chorus of mooing and bellowing from thirteen hungry calves. All of a sudden he couldn't remember what to do first.

"The list. I'll check the list," he murmured to himself.

First on the list was hay. "Right! I'll start with the hay. Maybe they'll stop mooing at me if I give 'em hay right away."

Hay had to be tossed down through holes in the floor of the hayloft, but Mr. Morley had thoughtfully left a stack of bales along the wall in front of the calves. Oliver tugged the strings off the first one and started passing it out to the hungry calves. One of them was bellowing. She had her leg tangled in the rope that hitched her into her stall, and when Oliver bent down to set her free, he felt something wet and scratchy tugging at the top of his head. "Yeeoww!" He pulled himself loose, tripped over a bale, and fell into the manger in front of the next calf.

Just as he was trying to figure out what had been after his head, he felt it again. He looked up. The calf was sucking his hair!

Oliver pulled himself loose again, wiped off his wet and slippery hair with the sleeve of his shirt, wrinkled his nose at the thought of being kissed by a hungry calf, and picked himself up.

When he had fed all the animals, he got the tin pot out of the calf-starter bag and gave them each a dish of grain. That went well, and he was whistling by the time he finished.

"I'd better clean out your stalls before I give you milk," said Oliver half to himself and half to the calves. "It's pretty messy around here." He grabbed the hoe and started scraping manure into the gutter. When he finished, he spread a nice thick layer of sawdust under each calf.

"Now for the milk." Mr. Morley had filled two pails at a time with the milk powder and water, so Oliver did the same.

"Here you are, ladies," he said as he held the

pails under the noses of the first two calves. They poked their heads into the pails and drank greedily. When they got to the last few drops, they made the same slurping sound as Oliver made when he got to the bottom of a milk shake. "Okay, ladies. It's all gone. Time for the next two."

Two by two Oliver worked his way down the row of calves. He had just two more to go before switching to the nipple pail for Number 13. "This is the easiest job I ever had," he thought as he held the pails for Numbers 11 and 12. "Easier than guinea pigs or ducks or rhesus—"

Suddenly and without warning one of the calves bunted the pail and sent it flying out of Oliver's hand. It landed, upside down, right in the gutter. "Hey!" he yelped. "Stop it!" Oliver bent down to pick up the pail. The calf bunted again. This time it was Oliver who went flying. He landed on his feet, but his feet landed right where he didn't want them to land. In the gutter!

"Oh, yuck! This is disgusting!" Oliver looked down at his feet. Then he looked at the calf who had put him where he was now standing. She gazed back at him and mooed softly, as if to say she was sorry. "You'd better be sorry," he muttered, stepping out of the gutter and scraping his feet on the floor to clean them off. "And that's it. You're not getting any more milk this morning." The calf mooed softly again. "All right, I know you're sorry. You can have more milk tonight."

Oliver set the two pails aside. Then he mixed the water and milk powder in the nipple pail

and took it to Number 13. "Okay, little lady," said Oliver, stroking her head and neck. "You're too small to bunt me, aren't you? Here's your milk."

Number 13 swung her head from side to side. She tried to back out of the stall. Then she jumped forward and gave a little kick with her hind leg. "What's the matter, Number Thirteen? What's making you nervous?"

Again Oliver held the nipple close to the little calf's nose. She sniffed at it and backed away. "Maybe she wants to drink from the top of the pail like all the others," Oliver thought. He put the pail on the floor and tried to gently push Number 13's head into it. But the calf was stronger than he'd counted on. She jerked her head out of the pail, spilling milk all over the floor.

"C'mon, Thirteen. You've gotta drink. You didn't do this when Mr. Morley fed you." But no matter how much Oliver stroked her head, no matter how sweetly he talked to her, Number 13 just would not drink.

Oliver left the barn telling himself that missing one meal wouldn't hurt the calf. "Maybe she's just nervous because she doesn't know me," he thought. "By tonight we'll be old friends. Then she'll drink her milk like all the others." But Oliver wasn't too sure.

As Oliver pedaled his bike along the road past Mr. Morley's fields, he thought about how the summer was going. "Good, and bad," he thought. The good part was that he finally had a job, and he was going to make some money. The bad part was that Number 13 wouldn't drink, and Oliver had no entry for the county fair. He could enter one of the contests that the other kids were in, but he really wanted to do something special—something original.

Oliver slowed down when he neared the fairgrounds, hoping to get some ideas. Workers were putting together a merry-go-round; others were erecting a huge tent; and over in the far corner near the cattle barns, several people were leading horses around a ring. Oliver stopped by the entrance. There were freshly painted signs, telling about the events that were not to be missed. One of the signs had the word "KIDS" in big red letters on the top line. Underneath it said:

**WE NEED YOU!
EARN MONEY AND HAVE FUN.
LEAD AN ANIMAL IN
THE CAVALCADE.
$1.00 FOR EACH ANIMAL.**

Oliver read the sign again. One dollar for each animal. It didn't say what kind of animal, so even Pom-pom would qualify. And more important, Oliver now had an entry for the fair!

Oliver smiled and pushed off on his bike. He had ridden about five feet when suddenly he slammed on the brakes, almost knocking himself off his own bike. "Wait a minute, Oliver Moffitt!" he yelled. "Wait just one minute now!"

Oliver turned his bike around and read the sign again. One dollar for each animal? He had fourteen animals in all! Thirteen calves and Pom-pom. He whistled under his breath. Fourteen! He could see it all now. Oliver Moffitt and his Thirteen Ladies, Plus One. "Wait until the gang hears about this," thought Oliver. "Won't they be surprised!"

"Won't Mr. and Mrs. Updegraff be surprised when they taste my Purple Worms pie?" Jennifer poured a whole bottle of purple food coloring into a bowl of cooked spaghetti and grape Jell-O. She mixed the strange-looking concoction with her hands. Purple splattered up her arms, down her shirt, across the table, and onto the floor.

Kim watched from a safe distance. She looked worried. "I sure hope that food coloring washes off. Otherwise Mom won't be too happy with this mess."

"Of course it comes off," said Jennifer, wiping her face with her hand and leaving a bright purple band across her forehead. "Besides, this is a prize-winning pie. One bite and the Updegraffs will say, 'This is a most unusual creation. It deserves first prize!' "

The Updegraffs were the judges for the food contests at the county fair. They were also the richest people in town. Mrs. Updegraff was very proper. She never smiled, and when she talked

she stuck out her chin and looked down at people.

Everywhere the Updegraffs went they took along their darling Tweetums. Mr. Updegraff always carried the little Yorkshire terrier while Mrs. Updegraff walked in front, holding on to the leash. It looked as if Mrs. Updegraff were leading her husband, not her dog.

Jennifer forgot about the Updegraffs as she poured her concoction into a pie dish. A blob spilled over the side of the dish and landed on the floor.

Kim picked it up. "Do you want this?" she asked. Purple Jell-O juice dripped off her fingers and ran down the length of her arm.

"Of course," Jennifer said. "Even a drop of Purple Worms pie is too precious to waste. Put it here."

Kim plopped the handful of dripping purple spaghetti into the middle of the pie. "Are you making a crust?"

"Oh, no. I don't need a crust. I'm going to chill it, and when the Jell-O gets hard, I'll be able to slice it into pie shapes. Neat, huh?"

"What's neat?" Jennifer and Kim wheeled around at the sound of Parnell's voice.

"My pie, of course," Jennifer answered. "How's that revolting creature, Squeeze Me, doing?"

"Great! C'mon up to my room and I'll show you."

"Are you kidding? I wouldn't come near your room. Not while that . . . that . . . thing is crawling around."

Parnell turned to his sister. "Kim. Tell your

43

friend that Squeeze Me is harmless, and he wouldn't come near anything purple."

Kim laughed. "Squeeze Me is harmless, Jennifer. Trust me. C'mon, let's go see him."

Jennifer stood on the bureau while Parnell put Squeeze Me through his paces.

"I've added an attraction," said Parnell, dangling a stuffed mouse on a string. "Squeeze Me has doubled his speed since I started dragging this in front of him. He'll do anything for a mouse."

Parnell put the boa constricter at the shoebox starting gate and pressed the button on his stopwatch. He dangled the mouse just in front of the snake's eyes. Like a cat after a canary, Squeeze Me followed the mouse. The moment the tip of his tail slithered through the last milk carton, Parnell pressed the button on the stopwatch. "Fifty-two seconds! A new track record!"

Parnell picked up Squeeze Me and hugged him. Jennifer shuddered.

"Nice going, Parnell," Kim said. "C'mon, Jennifer. We've got a mess to clean up."

On his way home from the barn, Oliver ran into Rusty. The neighborhood bully was polishing his bike on the front lawn.

"Hey, Oliver!" Rusty dropped the polishing cloth and quickly pushed his bike into the road, blocking Oliver's way. Oliver had to decide whether to put on the brakes or to run Rusty down.

Oliver decided to stop. Rusty leered at him.

"Well, look who it is! The only kid in town who's not going to enter a contest at the fair."

"Is that what you think, Rusty?"

"Yeah, that's what I think. That's what I know, Moffitt!"

"Well, maybe you're in for a surprise."

Rusty laughed. "Do you really think that you, Oliver Moffitt, could surprise me, Rusty Jackson? I'll bet you anything you don't have an entry for the fair."

Oliver drew himself up as tall as he could. "What do you want to bet?"

Rusty thought for a minute. "Okay, if I win a prize, you have to polish my bike every day for a week."

"And if I win a prize?" Oliver asked.

"Fat chance!" Rusty laughed out loud.

Oliver nodded his head. "All right, if you win a prize, I'll polish your bike every day for a week. But if I win a prize, you have to do my work for a week. That's the bet. Do you take it?" Oliver held out his hand.

Rusty grabbed his hand and pumped it up and down. "It's a bet, Moffitt. But if I were you, I'd practice polishing. I like my bike nice and shiny."

Oliver climbed back on his own bike and started to ride toward home. But from behind he heard Rusty call, "Hey Moffitt, just one more thing."

Oliver turned to see Rusty sniffing the air, and making a face.

"You stink!"

CHAPTER
4

"Oliver Moffitt, what's that peculiar smell?"

At the sound of Mrs. Moffitt's voice, Pom-pom came scurrying toward the front door where Oliver stood. The dog took one sniff and bounced backward as if his tiny feet were on springs. Pom-pom yipped and barked and practically turned himself inside out. The little dog sniffed Oliver again. Then in one bound Pom-pom leaped straight into Mrs. Moffitt's arms.

"Oliver! I'd like to know where you've been, and so would poor Pom-pom. Phew!"

"I've been doing my job, just like I told you."

"And what kind of job is that?"

Pom-pom wriggled out of Mrs. Moffitt's arms and slowly sniffed his way toward Oliver. Oliver bent down and held out his hands. "Wanna smell, Pom-pom? C'mon. It won't hurt you." As Pom-pom sniffed, Oliver continued. "I've been doing chores for Mr. Morley, the farmer who lives just past the fairgrounds. He's hired me for two weeks. I have to go every morning and night to clean them and feed them and give them—"

Mrs. Moffitt held up her hand like a police officer stopping traffic. "Hold it, Oliver Moffitt. Did you say 'them'? I thought we agreed on 'one customer at a time.'"

"But, Mom, I do have only one customer. Mr. Morley."

"Then who are the 'thems' you're talking about?"

Oliver took a deep breath. He knew he had to tell his mother the truth, but he also knew the truth might get him into big trouble. What if his mother wouldn't let him keep his job because there was more than one animal? What would he do? Mr. Morley was gone, and Oliver didn't know where he was. He couldn't just leave the calves by themselves. "I'm taking care of Mr. Morley's calves for two weeks. Thir-thir—" Oliver could hardly bring himself to say the next words. "Thirteen of them."

"Thirteen! Did you say *thirteen*?" The volume of Mrs. Moffitt's voice made Pom-pom scurry under the table and peek out from behind a chair leg.

"But I do have just one customer, Mom. Just like you said. I just didn't know my one customer would turn out to have thirteen animals. Honest, Mom. But Mr. Morley said I was a nice young man, and he's paying me grown-up wages because I'm doing a grownup's job. But I don't think he should pay me so much, do you?"

47

Oliver felt so nervous about what his mother might say that he couldn't stop talking.

"Oliver—"

"But, Mom," Oliver interrupted. "I'm not going to bring them home!" He concluded his case by lifting his left hand in a solemn pledge. "Animal Honor!"

Mrs. Moffitt looked at her son and shook her head. Slowly a grin spread across her face. "You've got a good head for business, Oliver," she said. "And I guess this is one time when thirteen really does equal one. Now, how about getting out of those clothes, on the porch, taking a shower, and we'll talk about your new job over breakfast."

"Thanks, Mom. I'm starving!"

Munching his way through a double stack of pancakes, Oliver told his mother all about his new job. "Everything went okay this morning except for one thing. Number Thirteen, the littlest calf, wouldn't drink her milk. I tried talking to her and petting her, but she still wouldn't drink."

"Well," said Mrs. Moffitt, "I don't know much about calves, but I do know that some animals get nervous around strangers. Maybe Number Thirteen needs to get used to you before she'll drink."

"I sure hope it doesn't take her too long. I want her nice and fat for the fair."

"The county fair?"

"Yes. I'm going to enter the cavalcade with my thirteen calves." Oliver didn't dare mention that he planned to enter Pom-pom too. He thought one surprise a day would be enough for his mother.

Mrs. Moffitt leaned back in her chair and folded her hands in her lap. "Funny you should mention the fair and the cavalcade. I haven't thought of that in years. I used to lead an animal in the cavalcade when I was a little girl."

Oliver's eyes nearly popped out of his head. "You *did*?"

"And I got fifty cents for it."

Oliver grinned. "I'm getting a dollar . . . for each animal." He paused. "And I'm going to give half of it back to Mr. Morley 'cause they're his calves, and without them, I wouldn't have anything to enter."

"That's very nice, Oliver. But I hope you won't forget Pom-pom during all this. Remember, he's your first responsibility."

"I won't forget good ol' Pom-pom. In fact, I think I'll take him with me tonight so he can get to know the calves."

"That's okay as long as he takes a shower, too, when you get home."

Oliver grinned. "You won't smell a thing, Mom. I promise."

When Pom-pom met the calves that night, it was as if they were long-lost pals. He sniffed their heads, and they sniffed his. He licked their noses, and they licked his. He yapped at them, and they mooed at him. Even Number 13 liked Pom-pom.

"There won't be any problem getting Number

49

Thirteen to drink her milk tonight," Oliver thought. "She's relaxed, and she's got a new friend."

But when Oliver brought her the nipple pail, Number 13 turned her head away. She mooed at Oliver and at Pom-pom. "You must be hungry, little lady," Oliver murmured as he patted her head and neck. "Why won't you suck?"

Pom-pom tried to lick Number 13's nose, but the calf bunted him and sent him flying into the manger.

"Hey! That's not nice," Oliver yelled, suddenly feeling sorry for Pom-pom, who was just trying to make friends. Then Oliver had an idea. Maybe Number 13 thought the milk was too hot.

He stirred the mixture with the long-handled ladle that Mr. Morley used. Then he took a spoonful, held it up to his mouth, and blew on it, just like he'd seen parents do for small children. "See, Thirteen? It's not hot." Oliver held the ladle close to his lips and pretended to sip the milk. Number 13 looked at Oliver and mooed. Oliver, still holding the ladle, bent down close to the calf's nose. He thought she was just about to take a sip when, from the manger in front of Number 13, a long-haired, moppy-looking creature leaped straight up and crashed into Oliver's arm. The milk-filled ladle sloshed right into Oliver's open mouth.

"Y-y-yuck!" Oliver yelled, spitting and sputtering and nearly gagging. "Look what you did, Pom-pom. You made me drink some of that stuff. Oh, gag! It's disgusting!" Oliver wiped his mouth on his sleeve and made a face as though he were going to be sick.

What was he going to do now? If Number 13 didn't drink soon, she'd never be ready for the cavalcade. And that was just the beginning of his problems. A skinny calf would never win a prize. No prize would mean bad news for Mr. Morley's farm. And what if Number 13 never learned to drink? Oliver gulped at the thought of Mr. Morley coming home and finding an empty stall where his prize calf used to be.

Everything was terrible. Just terrible. "C'mon, Pom-pom. Let's go home. We've got a problem, and I've got to think about it."

Oliver picked at the peas on his dinner plate and made roads in the mashed potatoes. "I've got to do something about Number 13, Mom. And I think I know what it is. I've got to go back to the barn tonight and stay there until she drinks. Even if it takes all night."

"All night? All alone? All by yourself?" his mother asked nervously.

"I'm not scared. Besides, I've got a reputation to keep up. Animals are my business. There's no job I can't handle."

"That may be true, Oliver, but I can't handle your staying out all night. You may go back to the barn tonight on two conditions. One is that you are home by midnight, and the other is that you take Pom-pom to protect you."

"Pom-pom's protection is like no protection at all," Oliver groaned. "And if it hadn't been for dear, sweet Pom-pom, I wouldn't have had to drink warm calf starter." The memory of the warm milk made Oliver feel like gagging all over again.

"Oliver!"

"Okay, Mom. I'll take him. But he'd better behave." Oliver could tell his mother wasn't about to back down, and besides, he thought it might be kind of nice to have some company in that big, dark barn all by himself—even if it was only Pom-pom.

It was nearly dark when Oliver sat the Shih Tzu in the basket at the front of his bike. As he set off in the direction of the Morley farm, Oliver hoped he wouldn't run into Rusty. But when he reached the Jackson house, there was Rusty on the front lawn, holding a giant slice of watermelon. Lined up a few feet in front of him were three cans into which he was spitting seeds.

Oliver nearly made it past unseen, but at the last minute Rusty spotted him. "Hey, Moffitt! Where you goin'? Want some company?" Rusty called.

Oliver pedaled faster. He didn't answer, and he didn't look back. The last thing Oliver wanted was Rusty Jackson's company.

Workers were bustling around the brightly lit fairgrounds as Oliver rode past. A circle of colored lights lit the empty Ferris wheel as it turned round and round. The riderless horses on the merry-go-round galloped up and down. Oliver felt a tingling in his stomach. Soon he would be part of the fair too. Pom-pom yapped at the people and the bright lights all around. "Yes, you too, Pom-pom. You'll go to the fair with me and the thirteen ladies."

Suddenly Oliver's tingling stopped. He remembered Number 13. "I've got to get her to drink that milk. It's my only chance to win a prize for Mr. Morley and to win my bet with Rusty."

Darkness had fallen by the time Oliver and Pom-pom reached the farm. Oliver pushed the barn door open and groped around inside for the light switch. Pom-pom whimpered. "Some guard dog you are!" Oliver said. "You're afraid of the dark!" Oliver felt a little afraid too and was glad to have someone to talk to. He felt around the wall some more until, finally, his hand hit the switch. He flicked it, and light flooded the barn. "Whew! That's more like it."

Except for Number 13, all the calves were lying in their stalls, chewing their cuds. Oliver thought they looked like their mouths were full of bubble gum—about five packages each. Number 13 mooed a long, deep moooooooooooooo. She swung her head from side to side and gave a little jump straight up in the air.

"Well, you're still feeling frisky, little lady, so why don't you drink your milk?"

Number 13 moooooooooooooooooooooooed again.

Oliver dumped a cupful of powdered milk into the nipple pail. He was about to add warm water, when he heard a thumping sound behind him. He turned around quickly, but all he saw was Pom-pom. "Did you make that noise, Pom-pom?" The little dog raised its ears and turned its head to one side.

"Must be hearing things," Oliver muttered. He turned on the warm water and started to fill

54

the nipple pail. Then he heard the noise again, this time louder and closer. It sounded like something—or someone—knocking on the door or the window. And now it was quietly moaning as well.

"Pom-pom! Stop it!" Oliver yelled.

Terrified, the little dog ran between Oliver's legs and whimpered loudly.

Oliver bent down and petted the dog. "Sorry, Pom-pom. I thought it was you making that noise. But if it wasn't you . . . who was it?"

Oliver's hands began to shake. He turned off the water, placed the pail on the floor, and nervously looked around. There were dark shadows everywhere. Bags of grain and bales of hay around the walls suddenly looked big and scary. Some even looked like they were moving.

"C'mon, Moffitt," Oliver said to himself. "Get hold of yourself. It's probably just the wind."

But as soon as Oliver had spoken those words, he remembered that there was no wind that night. Not even a breeze. He picked up the pail once more. Suddenly, from the darkest corner of the barn came a loud "Yeeooowww!" followed by a dull thud. Oliver's stomach dropped to his knees, and the pail dropped to the floor. Yapping frantically, Pom-pom took off in the direction of the "Yeeooowww!" Oliver tried to yell at him to come back, but no sound came out of his mouth, and his feet stuck to the floor in terror.

The pile of hay in the darkest corner of the barn slowly started to move. Pom-pom stood next to it, yapping so hard that his whole body

bounced up and down. From somewhere deep within the stack of hay came a muffled moan, like the moan Oliver had heard earlier, only even more frightening.

Oliver unstuck his feet and forced himself to walk—slowly—in the direction of the moving, moaning hay. What would he find when he got there?

Oliver shuddered and shuffled closer. The hay was still moving and moaning.

By the time he got close enough to see who or what had frightened him out of his wits, Pompom had climbed on top of the culprit and was licking his face.

"Call off your noisy little mop, Moffitt!" yelled an all-too-familiar voice.

Oliver's stomach climbed back into place. "So it's you, Rusty Jackson," he laughed. "I should have known."

Rusty pulled himself out of the hay and brushed it from his hair and clothes. "Okay, Moffitt," he spluttered. "You caught me this time. Or rather your dumb mutt caught me. But I had you scared, didn't I?"

Oliver puffed himself up to his full height. "You didn't scare me one bit, Rusty. I wasn't even nervous. But you're the one who's going to be nervous on the day of the fair—nervous about who comes out on top!"

"You don't have a chance, Moffitt. Not a chance. You don't even know what you're going to do yet!"

Oliver kept quiet for a minute. Then he said, "Go home, Rusty. I've got work to do."

Oliver watched Rusty climb onto his bike and pedal off into the night. Then he went back into the barn and finished filling the nipple pail with warm water. Pom-pom followed closely on Oliver's heels as he carried the pail to Number 13. The little calf still seemed quite nervous so Oliver stroked her head. "You must be getting mighty hungry, little lady." Oliver spoke softly to her. "How about some nice warm milk for supper?"

Oliver held the nipple close to the calf's mouth. She smelled it. "C'mon, please drink. Please," Oliver whispered. "Drink for me and for Mr. Morley and the blue ribbon."

A drop of warm milk oozed from the end of the nipple. Number 13 ignored it. Another drop oozed out, this time landing squarely on Pom-pom's nose. The little dog licked it off.

"You like that, huh, Pom-pom? Want some more? You might as well drink it, because it doesn't look like Number Thirteen is going to." Oliver held the nipple close to Pom-pom's mouth. First Pom-pom sniffed, then he licked, and then he grabbed it in his mouth and began sucking!

"Hey! I was just kidding, Pom-pom!" Oliver tried to pull the nipple from the little dog's mouth, but Pom-pom held on. "See, Number Thirteen. That's what you're supposed to do." The calf watched closely and mooed softly.

Oliver pulled the pail close to Number 13's mouth with Pom-pom still sucking greedily. "Look! Have you got the idea yet, Thirteen?" She mooed again.

"Okay, Pom-pom. That's enough." Oliver gave a tug, and the nipple slipped from the dog's mouth. Quickly he swung the pail to the little calf.

First she sniffed, then she licked, and then she grabbed it in her mouth and began sucking!

Oliver couldn't believe his eyes. "Yahoo!" he shouted. "We did it, Pom-pom! You showed her how, and we did it!" Oliver picked up the little dog and gave him a big squeeze. For the first time ever, Pom-pom licked Oliver's cheek, and Oliver didn't mind.

Number 13 was so hungry that after she finished the first pail of milk, Oliver gave her a second one. He let Pom-pom have another taste too. Then the tired farmer and the faithful guard dog pedaled home to their nice warm beds and to dreams of calves, and cavalcades, and a big blue-ribbon prize.

CHAPTER
5

"**Y**ou see, Oliver," said Mrs. Moffitt, "I knew Pom-pom was a very special dog from the moment I first laid eyes on him. You've misjudged him all this time."

"I have to admit he was a big help last night, Mom. You should have seen Rusty when Pom-pom was licking his face!" Oliver laughed as he remembered Rusty spluttering and thrashing around in the haystack. "And I don't know what would have become of Number Thirteen if it hadn't been for Pom-pom. I'll bet that's the first time a dog has taught a calf to drink!"

Mrs. Moffitt nodded knowingly. "I remember when I was growing up on the farm, we had a pig who thought he was a dog. He ran with the dog, he slept outside the doghouse, and he loved to eat dog food. But the funniest thing was, he chased cats!"

"Mom!"

"It's true! Scout's honor!" Mrs. Moffitt raised her hand in the scout salute.

"Well, since Pom-pom and Number Thirteen are such good friends now, I thought I might enter Pom-pom in the cavalcade too. As the shepherd dog."

"Pom-pom? A shepherd dog? I don't—"

"Please, Mom," Oliver interrupted. "All the calves like him, and I think he would keep them from getting nervous. Besides . . ." Oliver paused. "He might win a prize . . ."

Mrs. Moffitt's mouth opened, but no words came out. She looked down at Pom-pom sitting on her lap. Then she looked up at Oliver. "A prize . . .? Pom-pom . . .? Well . . . yes, I guess it might be all right. But just make sure you don't let him out of your sight, not even for a minute. In all the hustle of the fair, he could get scared. Or even worse—lost!"

"You can count on me, Mom." Oliver gave his mother a quick hug. "Now I've gotta run. I'm meeting the gang at Sam's this morning to talk about the fair."

In front of Sam's house Oliver saw something that made him slam on his bicycle brakes. Someone with Sam's hair color and Sam's body size and wearing Sam's clothes was half-hopping, half-jumping, half-running down the sidewalk. Beside her was someone else Oliver recognized. They clanked as they ran.

Oliver yelled, "Sam! What are you doing? And why is Andrew tied to your leg?"

Huffing and puffing, Sam and Andrew shuddered to a sudden stop. "We're in training for the three-legged race at the fair. Andrew's my partner. Aren't you, Andrew?"

Oliver looked down at the frowning boy. "He doesn't look like he's having much fun. And he's kinda short to be your partner, isn't he?"

"Yeah," said Sam. "That's why I tied the tin can to his shoe. But he's still not fast enough. I've got to think of something to speed him up. Got any ideas?"

Oliver shook his head.

Andrew looked up at Sam. "Jelly beans?" he asked.

Sam looked as if she was rapidly running out of patience. "Oh, all right, Andrew." She untied the strip of sheet holding their two legs together. Andrew flopped to the ground in a heap, until he saw the jelly beans.

"I'm going broke, but Andrew won't race unless he gets jelly beans." Sam sighed.

Oliver ruffled Andrew's hair and said, "Hang in there, Andrew." He turned to Sam. "Where's everyone else?"

"They're all inside, practicing. C'mon. Let's see how they're doing."

Happily munching jelly beans, Andrew followed Sam and Oliver to the front door. Just as they stepped inside, Parnell shouted, "Shut the door! Quick! Squeeze Me's escaped!"

Sam slammed the door behind them. "Where is he?"

Parnell clicked his tongue in disgust. "Sam! If I knew where he was, he wouldn't be missing, would he?"

Oliver quickly asked, "Where did you last see him?"

"Well, he had just set a new track record for the obstacle course—forty-nine seconds. Then I put him in this box, with this lid, in this corner." Parnell pointed to the box with one hand and held up the lid with the other. "Then I went to watch Josh and Matthew practice their karate moves. When I came back to check on him, Squeeze Me was gone!"

Josh, Matthew, and Kim appeared in the doorway. "We looked everywhere," they said.

"Where's Jennifer?" asked Parnell.

"Jennifer's on top of the piano," said Kim. "And we'll never get her down until we find your snake, Parnell."

"It's Squeeze Me I'm worried about, not Jennifer!"

"Well, Squeeze Me's got to be in the house somewhere," Oliver said. "Where does he like to hide?"

"In dark places," Parnell answered. "Behind things. Under things. Between things. How about if we each take a room and start searching."

"Good idea," Sam agreed. "Let's go!"

But before anyone had taken a step, an ear-splitting, blood-curdling scream pierced the air. The scream came from the next room.

The whole gang rushed in. They found Jennifer on top of the piano, screaming and pointing to a stack of newspapers.

"That . . . that . . . creature . . . That . . . that . . . monster . . . That . . . that . . . snake stole the fur ball from my shoe!" Jennifer screeched.

"Get that thief! Get him! Oh, I think I'm going to be sick." Jennifer put her hand to her mouth and made choking noises.

The front half of Squeeze Me stuck out from behind the pile of papers. The boa constrictor looked as if he had grown a furry purple beard.

"Oh, Squeeze Me," Parnell cried, rushing over to his pet. "Thank goodness! You're all right!"

"Thief! Thief!" Jennifer screamed again.

Parnell picked up the snake and gently wrapped him around his neck. Then he started to laugh. "Squeeze Me took your fur ball because he thought it was a mouse. He was only doing what any self-respecting snake would do after seeing something furry." Parnell gently pulled the fur ball from Squeeze Me's mouth and gave it to Jennifer. "Now, back in the box with you, Squeeze Me, and this time you won't escape."

Everyone watched while Parnell put the snake into the box and set six volumes of his encyclopedia on top.

"Whew! After all that excitement, I'm starving!" said Oliver.

"How about some Purple Worms pie?" suggested Jennifer, who had climbed down from the piano. "You all have to try a piece and tell me how it tastes. This is the eleventh time I've made it, and it gets more scrumptious every time!"

The whole gang gathered around the kitchen table while Jennifer took the pie from the refrigerator.

"I'm so hungry, I could eat a horse!" Matthew said.

"I could eat an elephant!" Josh added.

Oliver smacked his lips. "I could eat a horse *and* an elephant!"

"Well, you're getting Purple Worms pie," Sam reminded them.

Under her breath Kim murmured, "I hope everyone isn't *too* hungry."

Jennifer walked toward the table proudly holding the pie high in front of her face. But the pie was so high, she didn't see Andrew sitting on the floor in front of her and munching jelly beans.

Jennifer took a step toward the table. Then another step. Her third step landed on Andrew's leg. But it didn't feel like a leg to Jennifer. It felt as if she were stepping on a boa constrictor. A boa constrictor named Squeeze Me.

Jennifer leaped high into the air. The purple pie flew even higher.

Jennifer landed on the kitchen floor. The pie landed on Andrew's head.

"Oh, no!" Jennifer cried. "Now you won't get to taste my wonderful creation." She tried to scoop the pie out of Andrew's hair, but the spaghetti wriggled through her fingers and dribbled down his face.

Everyone stared at Andrew, whose face was now completely purple. No one knew what to say.

Andrew opened his mouth and stuck out his tongue. "Yum," he said. "Tastes like jelly beans."

Everyone laughed with relief. Finally Kim said, "Well, we know somebody likes it." Then she added, "Don't worry, Jennifer. I have to prac-

tice making my pie again, too, so let's make 'em together at my house."

"Good idea," agreed Oliver. "I wasn't hungry anyway."

"Me either," Matthew added. "Besides, I can't practice on a full stomach." He turned to Josh. "Right, coach?"

"Right. Wanna show 'em your stuff?"

"You betcha!" Matthew bent his knees, spread his legs, and raised his arms to neck height. From somewhere deep inside him came a series of grunts. "Huh! Hoh! Hah!"

Matthew advanced toward the kitchen table, slicing the air with rigid outstretched fingers. "Huh! Hoh! Hah!"

"How about a kick, Matthew," Josh suggested. "Show 'em your twirl-around-kick." Josh whispered to the gang, "This is the killer kick we worked out on the computer."

Matthew took a deep breath, inhaling until his chest looked like a balloon. He stared into space. He stood very still. "Huh! Hoh! Hah!" Matthew kicked high, twirled around fast—and landed flat on his back beside Andrew.

Andrew pulled a sticky, juicy purple strand of spaghetti from the top of his head. He offered it to Matthew. "Jelly bean?" he asked.

Everyone burst out laughing, even Matthew. Josh helped him up. "Back to the computer, Matthew. I think we'd better get the kinks out!"

Sam sighed a heavy sigh. "Guess we've all got some practicing to do before the fair." She turned to Oliver. "By the way, Oliver, I haven't heard you say that you were practicing. Haven't you thought of anything to do?"

Oliver cleared his throat. "I sure have. In fact, it sort of involves all of you."

"It does?" everybody asked.

"Well, let's just say that I'll need your help the morning of the fair."

"Doing what?" everybody asked again.

Oliver grinned. "Getting thirteen calves ready for the cavalcade."

"Thirteen *what*?"

Oliver looked at the surprised expressions on his friends' faces and laughed. Then he told them about his job at the Morley farm, and how badly he wanted to win the blue ribbon for Mr. Morley. He also told them about his bet with Rusty. "So you see, I'll need help getting the calves ready for the cavalcade. I want them looking their best, especially Number Thirteen. Can I count on you guys?"

The gang answered with one voice, "You sure can, Oliver!"

The day of the fair, Oliver got up with the sun. In the basket on his bike he stuffed brightly colored ribbons, combs and brushes, and on top of everything, he sat Pom-pom. When Oliver and his load arrived at the farm, all of the gang was there. "We're ready, Oliver. Put us to work," they shouted out together.

Once they recovered from the smell of the barn, they set to work brushing and combing the calves and tying ribbons and bows around their necks. Jennifer insisted on purple ribbons for her calf, Number 1. Sam tied a red bow around Pom-pom's neck and another one around each of his front legs. "Now the judge will *have* to notice *you*," she laughed. Pom-pom sat up on his hind legs, held out his paws, and yapped.

"The calves look like winners to me, Oliver," Josh said, "but how are you going to get all of them to the fair?"

"I'm going to tie them together in a line, with Number Thirteen bringing up the rear. And I'll tie Pom-pom to Number Thirteen, 'cause they're good friends now."

"We'll help you tie them together, Oliver," said Parnell, grabbing a rope. "Then we'd better get ready for our own contests. There's not much time left before Squeeze Me has to start slithering for gold!"

What a sight it was: Oliver Moffitt, president of Oliver's Pet-Care Service, leading thirteen gaily ribboned calves and one bow-tied dog down the road to the county fair. Everyone who saw them stopped and stared. Oliver smiled proudly. Everything was going so smoothly. "No problem," Oliver thought.

Oliver felt on top of the world. He could almost see the blue ribbon pinned to Number 13's halter. He imagined the judge shaking his hand. He imagined telling Mr. Morley about the prize. He imagined telling Rusty what chores he'd have to do. Suddenly Oliver stopped imagining. The *real* Rusty and his two sidekicks were riding their bikes right toward him and his parade of calves.

Rusty squealed to a stop within inches of the animals. They jumped and mooed and swung their heads from side to side and up and down. Several pulled so hard on the rope that they almost came untied. "Hey, Farmer Moffitt," Rusty hooted. "Wanna enter the stampede contest?"

Oliver ignored Rusty and spoke softly to the calves to keep them calm and quiet.

Laughing loudly, Rusty and his friends circled the animals and then sped off in the direction of the fair. Rusty yelled back over his shoulder, "Get ready for some bike-polishing tonight!"

When Oliver reached the barn with "calves" written over the double doors, he got another shock. Inside were dozens of calves and calf owners. "I won't have a chance!" he thought.

Oliver found the last empty spot in the far corner of the barn and tied up his thirteen Holsteins. He was just beginning to wonder when the cavalcade was supposed to start, when the head judge strode into the barn. The judge stepped up on a bale of hay and loudly cleared his throat. "Uh, ladies and gentlemen. It's nice to see so many contestants. May the best animal— and animal owner—win. I will now read the order for the cavalcade. Please remember who is in front of you."

Oliver listened carefully. The judge read name after name. No Moffitt. Could he have been left out? Why wasn't his name being called?

"And last, but not least," the judge chuckled,

"young Oliver Moffitt and his thirteen . . . ladies?"

"Whew! That was too close for comfort," thought Oliver. "But no problem. Now I'll have time to watch the rest of the gang in their contests."

He knelt down and petted Pom-pom. "You're the shepherd dog, Pom-pom. I'm leaving you in charge. Keep a close eye on the ladies." He stood up and stroked Number 13. "Whoever said thirteen was an unlucky number? Why, you're my lucky charm!"

Number 13 mooed softly.

Oliver strode out of the barn, whistling. "Boy," he thought, "this is a piece of cake! I hope the rest of this day goes as well."

CHAPTER 6

Oliver's skin tingled with excitement as he pushed his way through the crowded fairgrounds. Shouts and laughter mixed with the music of the Ferris wheel and the merry-go-round, the smell of hot dogs and cotton candy, and the voices of barkers inviting one and all to "step right up. Try your luck. Everybody wins a prize."

Oliver was about to step up and try his luck when suddenly he heard, "Oliver! Oliver! Over here!" Kim was waving her arms. "Matthew is about to do his karate. Hurry! You don't want to miss him!"

Oliver squeezed his way through the tightly packed crowd to where Kim and Jennifer were standing. "I haven't missed the Big Bake-off, have I?"

"No," Jennifer said. "It starts in about an hour, so that means we have time to watch everyone else."

The judge was just calling Matthew's name when they reached the karate demonstration platform. "From the A-Team, Matthew Farley. From the B-Team, Rock Richards. For the blue ribbon, Matthew will now attempt a never-before-seen technique, the Whirling-Dervish Drop Kick. And Rock will attempt to defend against it. Good luck, boys!"

"C'mon, Matthew!" Oliver shouted. "Show him your stuff!"

Matthew smiled and sliced the air with several quick karate chops.

Then, from the back row of the B-Team appeared Rock Richards. One glance at Rock, and Matthew's smile turned to stone.

Matthew was short. Rock was tall.

Matthew was skinny. Rock weighed at least 200 pounds.

Matthew was scared. Rock wasn't.

"Oh, no!" Kim, Jennifer, and Oliver gasped in unison.

Matthew looked over at Josh. His lips cried "Help!" but no sound came out of his mouth. Josh tried to look fierce and gave the thumbs-up sign.

The audience was silent with fear. Everyone held their breath.

Matthew looked out of the corner of his eye at Rock. He stood stiff-legged so his knees wouldn't shake.

Then, suddenly and without warning, from somewhere deep inside Matthew, came a sound: "Huh, Hoh! Hah!" It was the loudest "HUH! HOH! HAH!" that the A-Team had ever heard.

It was followed by the fastest karate chops and flick kicks that the A-Team had ever seen. Then Matthew twirled around three times, did a forward somersault, a back flip, and one last flick kick, which landed right in the middle of Rock Richards' stomach. Slowly, v-e-r-y s-l-o-w-l-y, all 200 pounds of Rock Richards sank to the mat. He landed with a THUD!

Matthew looked amazed by what he had done. The audience cheered and whistled. Rock Richards just lay there.

Josh rushed over to Matthew and pounded him on the back. "You did it! You did it! You won the prize!"

Matthew still looked like he couldn't believe what happened, but he managed a smile and said, "We won it, Coach. We won it together!"

"Great going, guys!" yelled Oliver. "Wish we could hang around, but we've gotta run or we'll miss Sam and Andrew. See ya later, winners."

The three-legged race had already started by the time Kim, Jennifer, and Oliver got there.

"There they are! They're winning!" Jennifer shouted, pointing to a pair of racers far ahead of all the rest. "But what's that funny-looking thing on the bottom of Andrew's foot?"

"Part of it is a tin can," Oliver said. "But the rest . . . ?" he squinted to get a better look. Then he started to laugh.

Jennifer nudged him with her elbow. "Well, what is it?"

"It's a roller skate! Sam said she needed to speed up Andrew, and I guess she's really done it!" Sure enough, strapped to the tin can on the bottom of Andrew's shoe was a roller skate. Andrew hardly moved his leg at all. He just glided along on the skate while Sam jumped, skipped, and hopped across the finish line.

Oliver cupped his hands to his mouth and shouted, "Good thinking, Sam!"

"First prize to Sam and Andrew!" called the judge. "The speediest three-leggers at the fair!"

"Congratulations," Jennifer yelled. Then she looked at her purple watch. "Hey! In a few minutes Parnell's racing Squeeze Me. We'd better get going, you guys!"

The Most Unusual Pet Contest was set up on the far side of the fairgrounds. To get to it, the three friends had to pass several other contests, including the Big Spit. Kim and Jennifer ran right past the event.

"Wait!" Oliver shouted. "I wanna see how Rusty is doing."

Kim and Jennifer stopped and turned around. "Okay, but let's make sure we don't miss Parnell."

Rusty and one other person, a girl about half his size, were standing side by side, holding slices of watermelon. "Our two contestants, Rusty and Suzie, will now compete in the final round," the judge was saying. He turned to Rusty and Suzie. "You have thirty seconds to see how many seeds you can get in the can. Ready? On your mark! Get set! Spit!"

Rusty sank his teeth into the watermelon, leaned as far forward as he could, and spit. He

missed. He took another bite. He spit again. He missed again. He looked down at Suzie. She was hitting the jackpot nearly every time.

Rusty waved his hand at the judge. "Hey! She's closer to the can than I am. It's not fair."

The judge laughed. "Suzie's the same distance away as you are, Rusty. You've only got five seconds left, so you'd better get spittin'! Five . . . four . . . three . . ."

Rusty got so nervous that his seeds went everywhere but into the can. "One!" The judge raced over to Suzie and pinned a blue ribbon on her shirt. Then he turned to Rusty. "Better luck next time, Rusty. But remember, there's nothin' wrong with winning second prize."

"Except that it's not first," Rusty muttered. He took the ribbon and pushed his way through the crowd. Oliver was hoping Rusty wouldn't see him, but he did. "See, Moffitt? I won! Just like I bet I would. Get ready for a week of polishing! Ha-ha-ha!"

For a second Oliver felt sick. Then he remembered his thirteen ladies waiting patiently for him back at the barn. "They won't let me down," he thought. "I know they won't."

Kim tugged at Oliver's shirt. "C'mon. We'd better hurry. Parnell will be very disappointed if we miss out on Squeeze Me's race."

When they arrived at the Most Unusual Pet Contest, a large crowd had gathered around Squeeze Me's obstacle course. Parnell was shouting, "C'mon, Squeeze Me, c'mon! Just two more boxes to go!" He pulled the stuffed mouse along in front of Squeeze Me. Then he checked his stopwatch. "Faster, Squeeze Me, faster!"

"I'll bet if that was a real mouse the snake would move even faster," a woman in the crowd whispered loudly.

A man standing beside her agreed. "Yes. And wouldn't it be funny if a real—"

"Mouse! A mouse! It's a *real* mouse!" the woman shrieked.

"Oh, no!" Parnell cried. The mouse belonged to the girl who had set up her Most Unusual Pet exhibit next to Parnell's. It was a somersaulting mouse, and by the look of things, the mouse had somersaulted right out of its cage . . . and right into Squeeze Me's mouth.

Parnell grabbed Squeeze Me, but it was too late. The mouse was history.

Parnell took a deep breath and walked over to the owner of the mouse. "I'm very sorry," he said. "I'll get you another mouse."

She shook her head. "There'll never be another Whiskers," she said sadly. "And your snake just—just *ate* him!"

"I'm afraid that's what snakes do."

She sighed. "I guess he was just doing what comes naturally—for a snake."

Parnell, the girl, and the rest of the crowd bowed their heads in a moment of silence. It seemed like a fitting tribute to poor Whiskers, the Somersaulting Mouse.

Then Parnell gathered up Squeeze Me. The boa wrapped around his neck and shoulders. "I think we'd better leave," he said. "We're sure to be disqualified for poor sportsmanship."

Parnell started picking up the boxes and cartons on the obstacle course just as the judge walked up. "You know, I've seen some very unusual pets today," said the judge. "But I've got to admit, the somersaulting mouse and that obstacle course were the two most clever ideas. So we've decided to offer a combined blue ribbon to you and to Veronica, the mouse's owner."

Parnell looked embarrassed. "I think you should just give the ribbon to Veronica, since Whiskers is now sort of combined with Squeeze Me."

Winning the ribbon brought a smile back to Veronica's face. "Are you sure you don't want to share it?" she asked.

"No," said Parnell. "This will be a lesson to us." He shook his finger at Squeeze Me. "You just can't go around eating your competition."

"Eating!" Jennifer suddenly spoke up, grabbing Kim's arm. "The bake-off! It's starting in five minutes! Let's go!"

Kim and Jennifer reached the bake-off table with just a few minutes to spare. They both stood proudly behind their pies while the judges, Mr. and Mrs. Updegraff, tasted their way through the other entries. Tweetums snuggled in Mr. Updegraff's arms. Finally, they came to Kim.

"And what is this called?" Mrs. Updegraff asked. She sniffed the pie.

"It's called Apple-Pan-Dandy," Kim replied. "I made it from my grandmother's recipe. It's traditional."

"Taste it, dear," Mrs. Updegraff said to Mr.

Updegraff. "Then tell me if I should taste it too."

Mr. Updegraff took a bite. "It's delicious," he said to his wife. "Yes, I think you should taste it."

Mrs. Updegraff tasted the pie. She smacked her lips loudly. "Why, you're right, dear. It *is* delicious. I think this Apple-Pan-Dandy deserves a prize. Don't you?"

Mr. Updegraff nodded. "Yes, dear. Anything you say, dear."

Kim smiled at them. "Thank you. My family will be very proud. It's our favorite recipe."

Mrs. Updegraff walked over to Jennifer. "And what have you made, young lady?" she asked, raising her chin and glancing out from under her glasses at Jennifer's pie.

"I've made an original creation," Jennifer began, proudly lifting the pie up so that Mrs. Updegraff could get a better look. "See?"

But as Jennifer picked up the pie, the Jell-O jiggled and the spaghetti wiggled. It looked like the pie had come to life.

Mrs. Updegraff gasped. "Oh, horrors!" she screamed. "Worms! Ogden, there are *worms* in that pie!" She pressed the back of her hand to her forehead. "It's too, too terrible. I . . . I . . . I think I'm going to faint."

Jennifer set the pie down on the table. "But, Mrs. Updegraff—" she began.

It was too late. Mrs. Updegraff was already beginning to slump to the ground. By the time Mr. Updegraff realized what was happening, his wife's head had nearly disappeared below

the table. Still clutching Tweetums, Mr. Updegraff lunged for his fainting wife. But as he lunged, his brand-new toupee slid off and landed in Jennifer's pie.

Now it was Jennifer's turn to shriek. "Eeeeek! There's a scalp in my pie! Get it out of here. Get that ... that ... hairy thing out of my Purple Worms pie!" But Jennifer didn't wait for someone else to get the toupee out of her pie. She grabbed it herself and flung it across the table. Everyone watched in amazement as the toupee glided through the air and landed on Tweetum's head. A terrified Tweetums jumped out of Mr. Updegraff's arms, yipping loudly and racing in circles.

By this time, Mrs. Updegraff was beginning to come to. "Worms ..." she moaned. "Purple worms." At last she was able to stand. She and Mr. Updegraff, followed by a hairy Tweetums, slowly made their way through the crowd and finally disappeared.

"Well, I guess that's that," Jennifer said. "No prize for me this year!"

"Sorry, Jennifer." Kim put her arm around her friend and gave her a hug.

Oliver, Sam and Andrew, Josh, Matthew, and Parnell all gathered around Jennifer. "That was the funniest thing I ever saw," Oliver said. "You may not have won a prize for the best pie, but you sure were the funniest act!"

"Thanks, Oliver. When does your act start?" Oliver looked puzzled. "What act?"

"You know. Your calf act. The cavalcade."

"Cavalcade!" Oliver shouted. "Wow! I almost forgot. I've got to get out of here!"

* * *

By the time Oliver and the gang reached the barn, the other contestants were moving toward the cavalcade ring. Because he was last in the parade, Oliver thought he still had plenty of time. But that didn't keep his stomach from doing little flip-flops every few seconds.

As he entered the barn, Oliver gazed at his calves all decked out in ribbons. "They look so beautiful," Oliver thought. "Just look at them standing there waiting for me to lead them to victory." He patted the head of Number 1 and led his ladies out of the barn.

"We'll cheer for you from the grandstand," Josh said. "Good luck, Oliver."

As the gang headed for the grandstand, Sam suddenly yelled, "Wait! Something's wrong here!"

Oliver whirled round. "What do you mean, Sam?"

"I mean, have you counted your animals? There are only twelve! Number Thirteen and Pom-pom are—missing!"

CHAPTER
7

All of a sudden Oliver's chest felt very tight. "That can't be!"

He ran to the end of the line. Sure enough, Number 13 and Pom-pom weren't there.

Oliver stared at Sam in dismay. "What am I going to do, Sam? What am I going to do?"

"You'll have to find them, that's all," said Sam. "I'll walk slowly with the other calves while you look."

Sam took the rope and started leading the calves toward the judge's stand. "You've only got about five minutes, Oliver," she called. "So hurry!"

"Thanks, Sam!" Oliver called over his shoulder. "You're a real pal!"

He ran for the barn, bumping into Parnell and the gang on the way. As soon as they heard the problem, they offered to help. "We'll look all around here," said Parnell.

Oliver reached the barn. But there wasn't an animal or person in sight.

"Pom-pom?" he called.

No answer—not even a yap.

Oliver searched the calf pens and stalls.

All of them were empty.

"Outside—maybe they're outside," Oliver told himself desperately. He burst out the back door.

But there was no Pom-pom and no Number 13. Oliver's shoulders sagged. How could they have disappeared all by themselves? Or had they? Maybe someone had dog-napped and calf-napped them. He might not ever see them again!

He imagined himself trying to explain when Farmer Morley realized that Number 13 wasn't around. Not only would he have no prizes to help the farm, he'd have lost the farmer's prize calf!

And then there was Mom. He could imagine her face when he tried to tell her that Pom-pom was gone forever. Oliver's heart sank to his shoes.

He dashed around, searching frantically in the bushes and behind the trees. Nothing.

Oliver stopped to wipe his forehead. In the distance he saw the barn where all the old-fashioned carriages were stored for the buggy parade. "It's a long shot," Oliver thought. "Maybe Number Thirteen came untied. Maybe she wandered into that barn. Maybe she dragged Pom-pom with her."

He sighed. "And then again, maybe not."

But he'd run out of other places to search. Careful not to get his hopes up, Oliver ran to the barn. It had no windows, so he couldn't look inside. He tried the big sliding door at the front, but it was closed. Oliver raced around to the back.

No Pom-pom or Number 13 hiding behind the barn. Maybe they were behind the cattle trucks. . . .

Oliver was just about to run over to them, when he stopped. He strained his ears. Was that a faint yap? It sounded as if it were coming from *inside* the carriage barn.

Pom-pom! Could it be Pom-pom? Oliver's heart thumped wildly in his chest. How could the dog have gotten into the barn? The door was closed. More important, how was *he* going to get inside?

Oliver ran around to the front of the barn again. Just as he reached the sliding door, he heard a loud voice coming from the loudspeakers. "We're getting near the end of the cavalcade, ladies and gentlemen. I can see our last entry in the distance. Oliver Moffitt and his thir . . . thir . . . Let me see."

The judge stopped talking. Then came a long silence. Oliver pulled frantically at the door. "Well, ladies and gentlemen, we're suposed to be seein' Oliver Moffitt and his Thirteen Ladies, but unless my old eyes are deceivin' me, it's *Olivia* Moffitt and her *Twelve* Ladies. But we have another minute or two before they reach the grandstand, so we'll do another count then. In front of me right now is Farmer Lawes and his two porkers, Lavinia and Lorelei. And mighty nice-lookin' pigs they are too."

"Can't waste time," Oliver thought. With all

his might he pushed against the sliding door. It didn't budge. Oliver pushed again, this time digging his toes into the dirt and putting his whole body into the job. Just as he was about to give up, the door squeaked open a crack. He slipped his hands into the opening and pushed against the door's edge. Slowly it slid back another two feet. Oliver peered into the quiet carriage barn. It was pitch black.

"Pom-pom? Are you in there?" he called.

No yap.

Oliver sighed. That was it, then. He must have been hearing things. He turned around, blinking in the bright sunlight.

From behind him came a faint and muffled yap. And it was answered by a soft *mooooo*.

Oliver whirled around, charging into the dark barn. He could hardly see where he was going. The carriages were just dim shapes. "Pom-pom? Number Thirteen?" he called.

Another *moooooo*. Oliver zeroed in on the sound—on the double! At the front of one carriage, with her ribbons still around her neck, stood Number 13. Oliver bent down and hugged the calf. Then he felt the rope. "Somebody tied you to this carriage, Number Thirteen. Who did this to you? And where's Pom-pom?"

Pom-pom must have heard his name. He let out the loudest and longest yap in Shih Tzu history.

"Inside the carriage!" Oliver yelled. He flung open the door, and in one flying leap Pom-pom landed in Oliver's arms.

"Oh, Pom-pom! You're all right. Am I ever

glad to see you! Who put you there anyway?"
His eyes narrowed. "Never mind. I can guess.
We've got to get you two out of here, and fast!"

Once again Oliver tied Pom-pom to Number
13. Then he led the dog and the calf out of the
dark barn and into the sunlight. The rest of the
gang spotted them and ran over. "You found
them!" Kim shouted.

"Yeah. I just hope it's not too late!"

"We'll cheer for you from the grandstand.
Good luck!"

In the distance Oliver could see Sam. Over the
loudspeakers he could hear the judge saying,
"Now it's about time for that Moffitt recount."

"Faster!" he whispered to Pom-pom and Number 13. "Faster!" Oliver started to run, pulling
the two animals after him.

"Let's see, now," said the judge as Oliver tied
Number 13 behind Number 12 and "Olivia" Moffitt slipped into the crowd. "One, two, three . . ."

Oliver's heart was pounding and he felt weak
in the knees.

". . . Eleven, twelve, thirteen." The judge
paused again. "Well, I guess you could say the
Moffitt entry has gone from twelve to thirteen
and a half, counting that furry-looking thing
tied to the end. Now, let's see who's leading
this parade. Yes, I do believe it's *Oliver Moffitt*
after all. Okay, son. Show us your stuff."

"Okay, ladies," Oliver whispered. "Show 'em
your stuff."

Loud cheers and whistles rose from the Purple Worms section of the grandstand as Oliver
led his parade past the judge.

"Looking good, Oliver!"

"C'mon, Oliver!"

"Yay, Oliver!"

"Huh! Hoh! Hah! Go get 'em, Oliver!"

The calves mooed, Pom-pom yapped, and Oliver smiled and waved to his fans. "This is great," he thought. "I just hope the judge thinks so too."

The judge spoke again. "Well, ladies and gentlemen. You've seen it all. That's the end of the cavalcade, and now it's time to pick the winners. We'll start with the calf section. There were so many entries that it's not easy for us to pick just one calf for the blue ribbon."

"Oh, please, let Number Thirteen be the winner," Oliver hoped. *"Please."*

The judge continued. "Usually the prize goes to the biggest, fattest, friskiest calf, but this year I've decided to award the blue ribbon to one of the smallest and youngest entries on the cavalcade. This calf is a real beauty. From the Morley farm and led by Oliver Moffitt, I'm pleased to present the first prize . . . and blue ribbon, to . . ."

Oliver held his breath and squeezed his eyes tightly shut.

". . . to Number Thirteen!"

The crowd was on its feet, cheering and clapping. And the loudest cheer of all came from Mrs. Moffitt, who had never before felt so proud of her son and Pom-pom.

"Yahoo!" yelled Oliver. Grinning from ear to ear, he marched proudly to the judge's stand and accepted the blue ribbon. He held it high over his head for all the crowd to see, especially Rusty. "Check this out, 'old pal,' " Oliver thought. "This beats your red ribbon. See you at the barn tonight!"

Oliver pinned the ribbon on Number 13's halter and started to lead the calves back to the barn. On the way he spotted Rusty. "Hey, Jackson!" he yelled.

Rusty pretended not to hear.

Oliver yelled again.

This time Rusty turned around. "Whadd'ya want?"

Oliver gave him his best smile. "I want to show you my *blue* ribbon. *First prize!*"

Rusty scowled. "So what?"

"So what? I won the bet, that's what!" Oliver paused, then added, "Even though you hid my animals."

"Er . . . um . . . me? Whadd'ya mean, Moffitt?"

"You know what I mean, Rusty. I found them in the carriage barn. *Tied up.* So I guess I'll see you at Farmer Morley's barn. Tonight. At seven-thirty."

Rusty turned and started to walk away.

"And one more thing, Rusty," Oliver called.

Rusty stopped and looked back over his shoulder.

"Don't wear your good shoes."

Oliver leaned against the old green tractor, his thumbs hooked in the belt loops of his jeans.

"You look just like a real farmer, Oliver!" said Sam.

He shifted the stalk of straw from one side of his mouth to the other, grinning at the gang.

"Yeah, Oliver, this is really neat!" Jennifer added. "A farm picnic for all of us."

"Yup," said Oliver. "Just as soon as I finish my chores." He leaned back and smiled as Pompom chased around his feet, yapping.

"Um, Oliver," Josh pointed out. "You haven't started doing any work yet."

Oliver grinned. "Farm work can be a lot of fun," he told his friends. "When you have the right kind of help."

From out of the barn door shuffled Rusty Jackson. He had a shovel over his shoulder— and a clothespin over his nose.

"Finished cleaning up in there?" Oliver called.

Rusty nodded. He was still holding his breath.

"Well, you'll be glad to hear that the next job will keep you out in the fresh air." Oliver pointed to a pile of paint cans. "The barn is looking a little beat up. It needs a new coat of paint. I'd love to stay and help, but I've got a picnic to go to."

He walked away with his friends. "You really won this time," Sam said.

"Me?" said Oliver with a grin. "I'd say Farmer Morley's the winner. He's got a blue-ribbon calf now. And soon he'll have a bright red barn for all the calves to live in!"